THEY THOUGHT
THEY SAW HIM

by
Craig Kee Strete

pictures by
Jose Aruego and Ariane Dewey

METROPOLITAN TEACHING AND LEARNING COMPANY

Watercolor paints and a black pen were used for
the full-color art. The text type is Geometric 231
Bold.

Metropolitan Teaching and
Learning Company Edition, 2000

ISBN 1-58120-969-X

1 2 3 4 5 6 7 8 9 10 CL 05 04 03 02 01 00

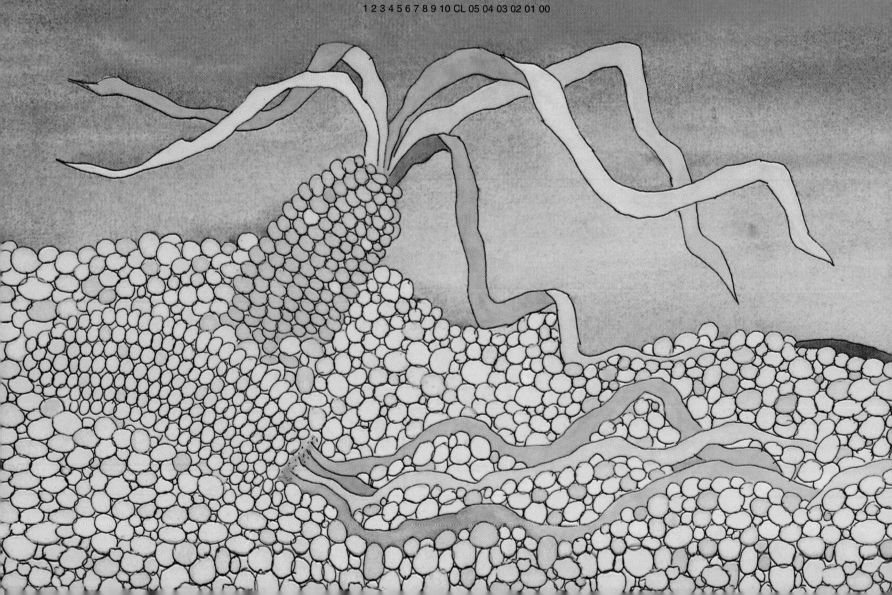

For Juan
—J. A. and A. D.

Little dark chameleon crept out of the heart of his winter home and moved up onto a tiny branch.

Rain puddles glistened beneath his feet. The wind blew warm over the walls of the adobe. All winter little dark chameleon had lived, safe and asleep, beneath the granary where the people kept their seed corn.

Now insects buzzed over bush and tree, and he was awake.

As he moved on quick, silent feet, he began to forget the sleepy winter dark and felt now the joy in the first wakeful light of spring.

Eyes half closed, still filled with winter memories, little dark chameleon sat on a brown branch and waited for an insect to find his tongue.

A hungry snake watched him. The snake climbed the tree to catch the dark chameleon for his first meal of the spring.

But when he got there, everything on the brown branch was brown.

"The dark chameleon got away," said the snake, and he slithered off.

Little brown chameleon jumped off the brown branch. His feet gripped green leaves, and he hung there. His sticky tongue caught a bug.

An owl, flying home to sleep, saw the brown chameleon in the green leaves. The owl swooped down to catch him.

But when he got there, everything in the green leaves was green.

"The brown chameleon got away," hooted the owl, and he flew off.

Little green chameleon jumped out of the green leaves
and landed softly in the tan, rain-washed sand.

A fox saw the green chameleon in the sand. With pointed ears and hungry eyes, the fox crept toward him.

But when he got there, everything in the tan sand was tan.

"The green chameleon got away," yipped the fox, and he ran off.

Little tan chameleon crawled up on a ridge of golden rock.

An Apache boy saw the tan chameleon and tried
to sneak up and catch him for a spring surprise.

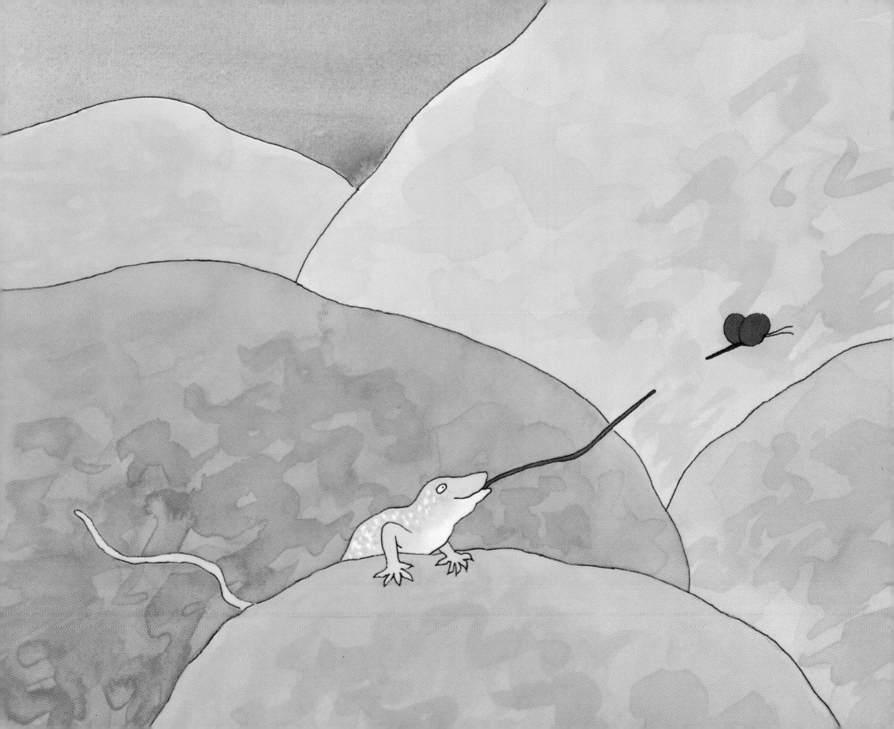

But when he got there, everything on the golden rock was golden.
"The tan chameleon got away," said the boy, and he slowly walked off.

Little winter-dark, brown, green, tan, and golden chameleon
warmed himself in the sunlight.
Snake, owl, fox, and boy all thought they saw him.

But little chameleon had his secret.

"Nobody sees me," he said, "because I am the color of the world."